The Talking Vegetables

Retold by **Won-Ldy Paye** & **Margaret H. Lippert**

Illustrated by **Julie Paschkis**

Henry Holt and Company ● NEW YORK

ABOUT THE STORY

The Talking Vegetables is a traditional story from the
Dan people of northeastern Liberia. Every Dan village
has a community farm, and everyone works hard to
make this farm a village treasure. When somebody in the
village gets sick, friends pick vegetables from the farm
for the family. When there is an important celebration,
villagers harvest vegetables from the farm for everyone
to enjoy. Dan parents and grandparents will often tell
children *The Talking Vegetables* to remind them that they
are important members of their families and that their
work is needed so the community will thrive.

Henry Holt and Company, LLC
Publishers since 1866
175 Fifth Avenue
New York, New York 10010
www.henryholtchildrensbooks.com

Henry Holt® is a registered trademark of Henry Holt and Company, LLC.
Text copyright © 2006 by Won-Ldy Paye and Margaret H. Lippert
Illustrations copyright © 2006 by Julie Paschkis
All rights reserved. Distributed in Canada by H. B. Fenn and Company Ltd.

A version of this story was previously published in *Why Leopard Has Spots:*
Dan Stories from Liberia by Won-Ldy Paye and Margaret H. Lippert,
illustrated by Ashley Bryan, by Fulcrum Publishing, Inc., Golden, Colorado, 1998.

Library of Congress Cataloging-in-Publication Data
Paye, Won-Ldy.
The talking vegetables / retold by Won-Ldy Paye and Margaret H. Lippert;
illustrated by Julie Paschkis.—1st ed.
p.   cm.
Summary: After Spider refuses to help the villagers plant the vegetables,
he is in for a surprise when he goes to pick some for himself.
ISBN-13: 978-0-8050-7742-1 / ISBN-10: 0-8050-7742-1
1. Anansi (Legendary character)—Legends. [1. Anansi (Legendary character)—Legends.
2. Folklore—Africa, West.] I. Lippert, Margaret H. II. Paschkis, Julie, ill. III. Title.
PZ8.1.P28Tal 2006   398.2'089'9634—dc22   2005019757

First Edition—2006 / Designed by Laurent Linn
The artist used Winsor & Newton gouaches to create the illustrations for this book.
Printed in the United States of America on acid-free paper. ∞

10 9 8 7 6 5 4 3 2 1

To Alden,
my wife,
for laughing with me
—W. P.

For Margie
MacDonald
—M. H. L.

To Daisy and
Gus Emminger
—J. P.

BAM! BAM! BAM!

"Who's pounding on my door so early in the morning?" Spider shouted.

"Your neighbors. It's time to clear the land for our village farm."

"Go away," said Spider. "I'm tired."

"But we need you," they said. "If everyone helps, there will be plenty of vegetables for all of us."

Spider yawned. "I don't need your vegetables. I have plenty of rice."

Everyone in the village walked down the road to a clearing in the forest.

Everyone except Spider.

They worked all day cutting down bushes, tearing out vines, and digging up roots. They raked smooth beds and built a waterway.

The next morning, the villagers came again to Spider's door.

BAM! BAM! BAM!

"Who's there?" Spider called.

"Your neighbors. Come help us plant the seeds."

"I said **no**, and I meant **no!**" shouted Spider. "Now **go away!**"

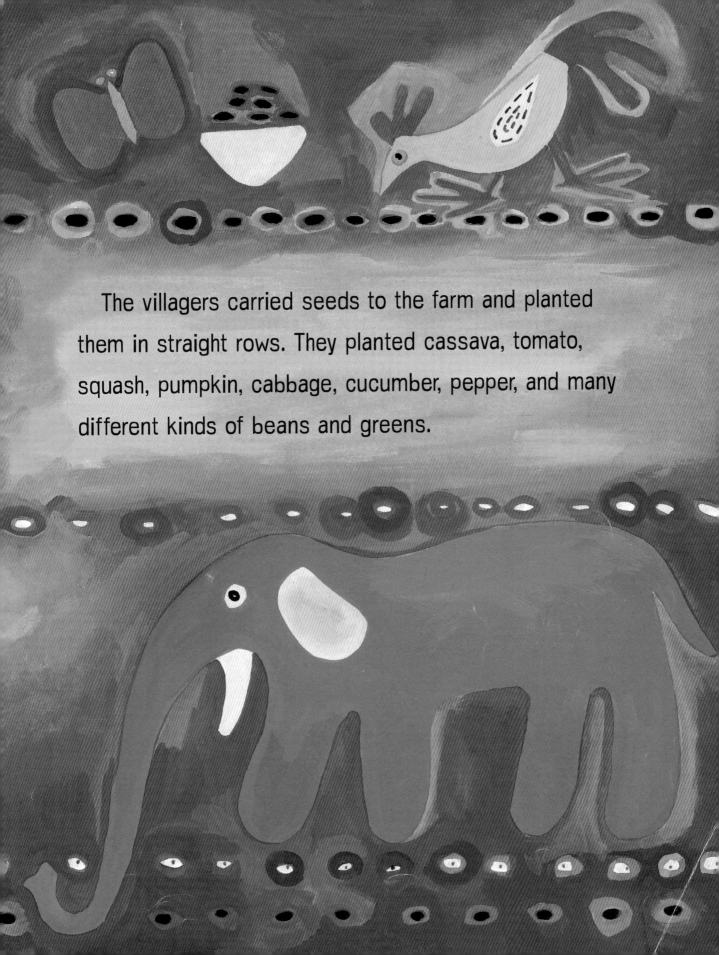

The villagers carried seeds to the farm and planted them in straight rows. They planted cassava, tomato, squash, pumpkin, cabbage, cucumber, pepper, and many different kinds of beans and greens.

A month later, the villagers knocked on Spider's door again.

BAM! BAM! BAM!

Spider opened his door and yelled, "What do you want **now?**"

"It's time to weed the farm," they answered.

"I didn't help before, and I'm **not** helping **now!**" Spider screamed. He slammed the door and went back to bed.

All day the villagers pulled weeds. Their knees hurt, their backs ached, and their arms were sore.

In time, the vegetables began to ripen. The villagers
picked what they wanted.

One day Spider said to himself, "I'm getting tired of rice. Plain rice, day after day after day. I live here. I'm part of this village too. I'm going to pick myself some vegetables to go with my rice."

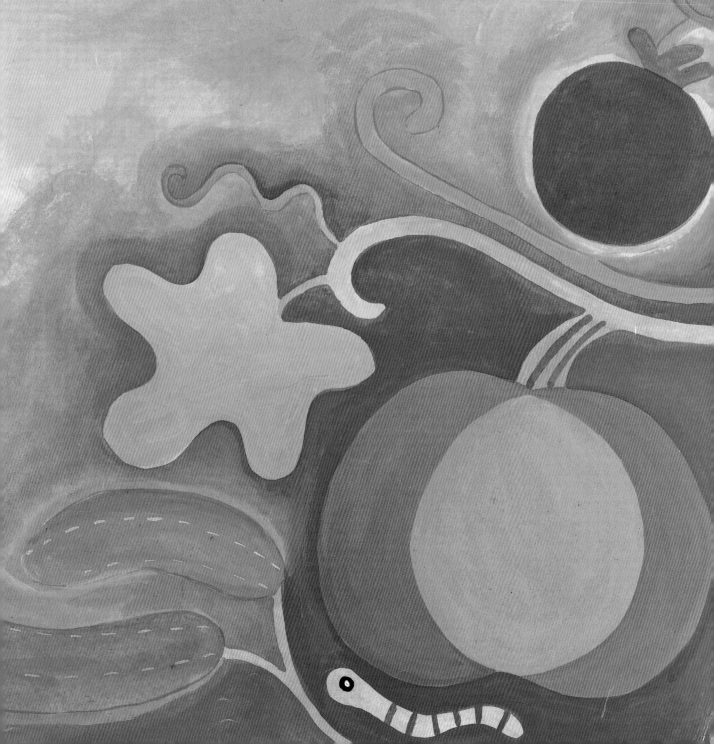

When Spider got to the farm he couldn't believe his eyes. Huge cucumbers lay on the ground. Giant pumpkins rested under green leaves. Juicy tomatoes hung from vines.

"**Wow!**" said Spider. "Those tomatoes look delicious. I'll just take one, or maybe two."

Spider reached out to pick a tomato from the nearest plant. The tomato shook itself and said, "What are you doing?"

Spider said, "Wha . . . ? A talking tomato?"

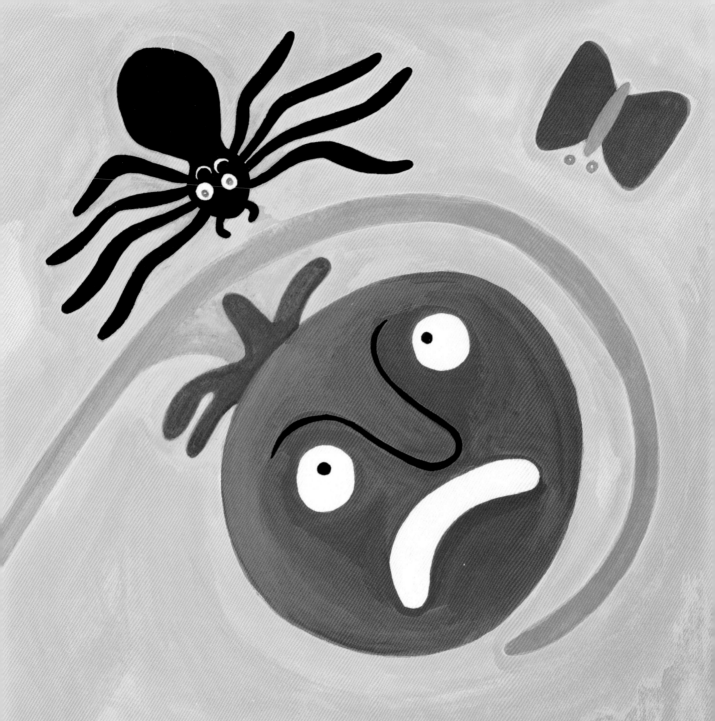

The tomato said, "Why do you think you can pick me when you didn't come to clear the land or plant my seeds or pull the weeds? Get out of here!"

Spider backed away. He looked around and said, "There are so many fat cucumbers on that vine. I'll just take one, or maybe two."

But as he walked toward the cucumber vine, it started moving away from him. Spider was surprised. He'd never seen a moving vine before. It twisted all over the ground.

"**You** can't pick us," said a cucumber. "You didn't clear the land. You didn't plant our seeds. You didn't pull the weeds."

Spider ran to the other side of the farm. Ahead he
saw a perfect pumpkin—big enough, but not too big.
"I'll just grab that pumpkin on my way out," he said.
But he couldn't lift it. The pumpkin stuck to the ground.

He tugged and pulled, but the pumpkin wouldn't move. "**You** can't take me," the pumpkin said. "**You** didn't help make the farm. **Go away!**"

Spider tried to find his way out of the farm, but the vegetables reached up to grab him. Leaves covered his eyes. Stems stretched out to trip him.

Spider finally got free. He ran all the way
back to the village.

When he got home he was tired and hungry. He put a pot of water over the fire and boiled some rice.

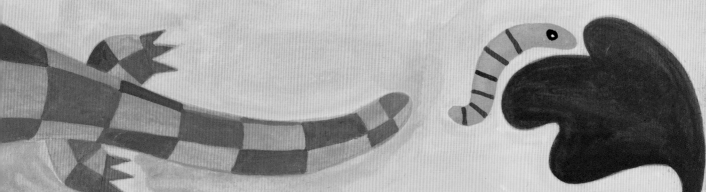

That night he ate rice for dinner.

Plain rice!